Broken Chain

The River's End

Joe Cundiff

To Augie,

Joe

Published by NeMours Publishers, LLC
Copyright © 2019 Joe Cundiff
Cover Art and Graphics by Jacqueline Frackelton
Cover Photography Contributions by John Hafner Photography
http://johnhafnerphotography.com/
Cover Photography Contributions by Joe Cundiff
http://joecundiff.com/
Editors: Timothy Sams, Jenny Yonkman-Bangma
Author pages: YouTube.com/joecundiff
@joecundiffauthor

ISBN-13: 978-1090450760

DEDICATION

The River's End is dedicated to my readers, this really is for you. I hope you enjoy this magical journey and thanks for running along with me on this epic adventure. It means a lot!

.

CONTENTS

ACKNOWLEDGMENTS

As with any endeavor of passion, there are simply too many people to list. So, to all of my friends and family that have offered support and words of encouragement throughout this journey, I can only say thank you! You all made this happen.

And to my daughters, Jordyn and Jayde, thank you for always believing in your dad. Love You!

To my Editor in Chief, Tim Sams, there are not enough words. I simply would not be here as a writer without your help, and this book would have never made it to print. You pushed me, encouraged me and made me believe that I am a writer. You are a gentleman and a friend. Thank you, Sir!

To Jackie Frackelton, my favorite artist and dear friend, this too would not have happened without you and your (and David's) support. Once I shared my vision for the cover, your graphic magic and artistic touch brought this story to life. Thank you for all of the creativity and patience. A true work of art!

To Chad Corbett, we shipped it my friend! More than anyone, you pushed me to make this dream real, to focus on the outcome, to add value first, and to chase the feeling. Thank you my friend.

And to Jenny Younkman-Bangma, my number two editor, but never second place. Your insights and encouragement took me to the finish line and helped make this book a reality. Thank you so much, but we still have work to do!

Special thanks to Author Alan Janney for the idea to write these bonus chapters.

Joe Cundiff

FOREWORD

BROKEN CHAIN – THE RIVER'S END

The journey that began as a simple short story about a dog unfolded into an epic tale of friendship and adventure, and then somehow it evolved into a book and my first novel: *Broken Chain – The Echo of Lone Howls*. While writing this book, I often found my fingers chasing the keyboard, trying desperately to keep up with Biggs & Cota as the action rolled across the screen. Hopefully, you enjoyed reading *The Echo of Lone Howls* as much as I enjoyed writing it.

If you loved romping the rivers and woods with Biggs & Cota, (and miss them already) then you will love this trek, deeper into the woods, for more 'behind the scenes' action. *The River's End* will be the perfect remedy. But first, let me tell you how writing this second book came about. It was during a front porch conversation (on rocking chairs of course) with my friend and neighbor, author Alan Janey, that the idea for the bonus book emerged. Alan suggested that my readers might want to know more about Biggs & Cota, and perhaps, I could offer a different perspective. And more action.

So, I went home and pondered that advice for a few days, then stared writing. Once again, my fingers struggled on the keyboard, trying to keep up with the action. *The River's End* takes us back to a time Before the Bowl, and offers a glimpse into the early life of both Biggs & Cota, but it does not end there. This time Cota leads us through a tireless journey, with an in-depth view through the lens of a coyote.

Come run along as Cota weaves through the backstory of many of your favorite scenes from the first book.

~joe

Joe Cundiff

The River's End

29

BEFORE THE BOWL
BIGGS & COTA

*I am Cota, legend of the Lone Howls. By now, you have heard
of me and know some of my story. I am here to tell you more, to
tell you about my first encounter with Biggs, and how I came to
track the warrior German shepherd. You know him too, but
you don't know all.*

~ Cota

Cota seldom spoke, but when he did, his words hung in the air
as if time may end with his next breath. Both his tone and
demeanor fueled the gravity of importance to his words.
Cota's voice was soft and gravely, like the whisper of a
thousand souls.

But something was awry with Cota and suddenly his words
came sharp, and fast.

"Have you seen Biggs!?" Cota asked excitedly, but already
knowing the answer.

Bear's head moved slowly, side to side, confirming Cota's fear.
Biggs had not been seen or heard from since the great wind
storm swept through the Farm. Still, Cota felt safe confiding
in Bear, though not sure why. It was odd enough that Cota
had befriended a German shepherd. Now he was perched on
a boulder, eye-to-eye with a five-hundred-pound black bear,
and somehow it seemed okay.

Biggs had been gone for weeks. The humans called it a
tornado, and Biggs's Master feared that his dog was dead,
swept away by the powerful funnel of wind. Cota had watched

as Master searched for days for his prized dog, but Biggs was nowhere to be found. Forced back to the work of cleaning up the Farm and repairing the Barn, Master had not given up on Biggs, but he had lost hope.

Cota believed his friend was still alive.

After a long pause, Bear finally spoke, "He would have come back by now if he was alive. This is his home." Bear believed that Biggs was dead.

Cota sat silently, dejected for the moment by Bear's disbelief. But, the feeling in his gut was too strong. "I know he is out there!" Cota retorted, surprised by his own boldness in the face of the massive Bear.

Bear tried to speak softly, but his voice clawed from the grains of a deep wooden drum, resounding soulfully into the darkness. His sharp bellowing growl interrupted the calm of a windless night. "If he were alive, why would he not come back? Makes no sense."

Cota sat quietly again as the echo of Bear's words sifted through the damp fog. He was mad that Bear did not believe Biggs was alive. Cota could not explain it, but the feeling he had was real. *Biggs is out there!* He thought. *And he needs our help.* Cota could not understand why Bear did not feel it too, and he was determined to convince him, whatever the cost.

Each night for the past week, both Bear and Cota had been separately lurking in the darkness of the woods surrounding the Farm. Finally, Cota had summoned the courage to approach Bear. "If you think he's dead, why do you come here every night?" Cota snapped at Bear.

Bear spoke defiantly and with authority. "The first night I came hoping Biggs would be here--or at least hoping to find some sign of him. I kept coming back each night, thinking it might be different. But last night, it all changed and I knew he was gone for good."

"Why?" Cota barked angrily.

"Have you seen the broken chain?" Bears words were heavy, like the darkness, and hung in the air like the weight of a thousand iron links.

Cota sighed, a long exasperated breath, then lowered his head. "Yes. I saw the chain."

Both Bear and Cota, at separate times and beneath the veil of darkness, had ventured onto Biggs's sacred circle of dirt, to search for any sign their friend might still be alive. What remained of the chain still lay in a coiled heap, one end still attached to the old wheel axle and bound in a mess of tangled barbed wire. The other end was missing three-feet of links and the dog that had once been attached. The one severed link that had succumbed to the twisted torque lay atop an old oil drum next to the barn. Master had found the link lying on the ground near where Biggs's dog house once stood.

Cota already knew about the link, he had been lurking in the woods and saw Master bend down and pick it up. He studied it close, then gripped it tightly in his hand. Master's eyes filled with tears as he ambled toward the barn. He set the mangled link atop the oil drum and kept walking. The link was still there, a troublesome reminder of the brutal force of winds that had ripped the roof completely off the Barn and splintered trees for miles. The tornado that had swept Biggs's house away and any hope that he might still be alive.

"No way he could have survived that wind. It ripped the roof off the barn and snapped his chain apart," Bear said painfully.

Cota knew that all the evidence was working against him. Still, Cota believed that Biggs was alive.

In the distance, a train's horn blared through the darkness, followed by the rumble of rolling steel. Cota had heard the sounds of trains so often that he seldom gave them a thought. But this time, it was different. There was a mysterious meaning to rumbling rhythm. Cota was drawn to the beckoning of the iron stallions. The train was trying to tell him something, he just did not know what. *The train knows!* Cota thought.

Cota was now standing atop the rock, ready to bound into action. He had no idea where to begin, but the train was calling, sending a message that Biggs was out there. Somewhere!

"We need to go find him!" Cota barked sharply. "He might be in trouble! He might need our help!"

Bear was immovable. The large black mound rose up, standing tall on his hind haunches and towering over the moment - as if his presence needed to display any more authority than his voice already had. Then he calmly sat down, rolled his head, and cast his dark, steely eyes toward Cota.

"He's dead," Bear insisted.

Cota met his stare, then sat back down. Bear's eyes pierced Cota's soul and wounded him more than the absence of Biggs. Cota was afraid to speak or even move. Once again, Cota was all alone.

Bear's long curved claws glistened in the damp darkness, and Cota's mind drifted to his first encounter with Bear.

***

Cota had tried to slip in around the napping Bear and steal a bite of discarded fish. But his cunning and stealth had proven nearly fatal. Just as Cota was about to clamp down on his next meal, Bear snorted in the scent of the coyote and his senses roused him from a deep slumber. It was the first time Cota had locked eyes with a bear and he'll never forget his wide-eyed, piercing stare of death. He'll also never forget how stunningly fast the big black mound could move. Cota instantly darted away and was in a full-stride sprint as quickly as his paws could grab the earth. Bear rolled over, dug his hind legs into the dead fall of a tree, and lunged at Cota.

The wide swooping arm of Bear swept Cota off his feet and sent him spiraling into the air. Bear's claws just missed Cota's torso, or he would have been ripped to shreds in one fatal blow. Luckily for Cota, just as he bound over a rock, Bear's claws slashed beneath his belly. The forearm of Bear connected with Cota's hind haunch and sent him tumbling. Cota rolled out of reach and scrambled to his feet, then disappeared. Bear never gave chase, but rather turned over, devoured the fish and went back to sleep.

Cota never mentioned the incident, but he was certain Bear remembered him.

***

The memory of their first encounter raced through Cota's mind as he sat mere feet from Bear. Cota braced for either a death swat from Bear's long claws--of which he was too close for an escape--or for the profound wisdom that was certain to come from Bear's next words. Nothing could have prepared him for what came next.

"Tell me how you and Biggs became friends," Bear asked casually, as if they had all night to talk. "It is unusual you know, for a coyote and a human's dog to be friends."

More silence. Cota wanted to go find Biggs, not tell stories, but Bear was immovable. Cota relaxed a bit, caught his breath, then suddenly had an itch and his hind leg dug rapid-fire into his neck until it passed. He stood again on the rock and shook the loose fur into the air. His feet slipped on the damp moss, but he quickly recovered and managed to stay atop the boulder. Finally, Cota stopped all the commotion and stood with his head crouched low in a cowering stance. His eyes met the piercing stare of Bear.

It was painfully apparent that Bear was not amused by the nervous fidgeting of the coyote. Slowly, Cota sat down, straightened his back and looked at Bear defiantly. Bear sat up a little straighter and looked down at Cota, even though he was perched on the boulder, and said, "let's hear it!"

Cota's defiance succumbed to the thunderous cloud of Bear's command. He took a deep breath, looked off into the darkness and began to speak. The words soon flowed and the fondness he felt for both Biggs and the Farm surprised Bear. Cota still wanted to be mad at Biggs, after Master had tried to kill him. But telling his story changed all of that. Saying it all out loud, Cota was surprised by his own admiration of Biggs.

***

"It was just after my second winter when I first came here, to live in the woods around the Farm. I had wandered alone for days. It was during the warm months, and I was still very angry. My only sister, Willow, had left me to join another pack, and I wanted to get far away from the place where I was born. Only bad memories there. Anyway, after I crossed the mountain (Cota pointed his snout toward the south and the highest peak, a silhouette touching the dark sky) and swam through the East River, I ended up in the lowlands beyond the Sadie Hollow."

"The ground was soft from all the rain and I was tracking a small herd of lost cows. There was no path or other prints as they forged through heavy brush. I followed them into the swamps, so I knew they were lost."

"The cows had escaped the Farm. I figured it all out later when I tracked back. A tree had fallen across the fence, and the cow tracks went right across it. Anyway, there was one young calf, only a few months old, and she was struggling to keep up. The deeper they tracked into the swamps, the better my chances of eating. I was hungry, of course, and she was going to be an easy kill."

"I had tracked them through the night, hoping the little one would fall behind, far enough for me to strike. They were lost and anxious, and never had a clue I was there, not even the momma. When they got to the swamp, the group trudged through marsh and mud. But the little one stopped at the edge. She was bawling for her momma. Momma was belly deep and her legs sunken in the murk. It was too deep for her to quickly turn and get back to the calf."

"This was my chance to strike!" Cota's voice grew louder. "I had started down the ridge and was about to sprint in and pounce on the helpless calf. But then I heard a human voice. Then I heard Biggs's bark for the first time!"

"I darted off to the right, away from the voices, and trekked back around the back side of the ridge. They never saw me, of course."

"From up high, I looked down and there he was. Biggs was younger than me. But his bark was not like the sharp, high pitched nipping of a pup. Rather, it was deep, and intimidating. I was both surprised and impressed."

"I watched it all from the ridge. It was crazy!"

Bear was suddenly intrigued by the coyote turned storyteller. "Then what happened?" Bear demanded.

Cota got caught up in his own storytelling and barely flinched at Bear's anxious command. Instead he paused and stared into the darkness, his mind drifting back to the swamp. He recalled every detail.

"I moved along the ridgeline without being noticed. They had no clue I was watching."
"Who?" Bear asked. "The cows? Biggs?"
"Yes, and Master, too," Cota replied.
"Master was there?" Bear asked.
"Biggs was yapping his head off! 'Over here! Over here! Over here!' Until Master finally caught up. He came slipping and stumbling in the mud, then stopped and bent over breathing hard. They must have been looking for the cows a long time," Cota's voice growing with excitement.

"Anyway, I heard Master say, 'That's a good boy, Biggs! Good Boyha!' That's when I learned his name." Master went on bragging about how Biggs was going to make a great farm dog. Biggs had tracked the lost cows deep into the swamp, and he was only a pup! That's what Master was going on about."

"Is this what you call crazy?" Bear asked with growing irritation.
"No, I'm trying to tell you," Cota said even more annoyed.
"Let's hear it!" Bear demanded.

Cota gathered himself and continued. "Biggs was still yapping, but this time at the cows. He was circling the edge of the swamp, trying to get them to go out the other end. It was like he had done it a hundred times. At least that's what Master said."

Bear looked at Cota with growing disdain.

Cota squinted his eyes and looked rebelliously at Bear, then told more. "Master stumbled around the back side and scooped up the calf in his arms. I was so mad. I was so hungry."

"Anyway, I tracked along the ridge and watched as Biggs herded the cows out the bottom and back toward the Farm along the logging trail. Master carried the calf up from the swamp and put her on the trail. She bawled the whole time, and my stomach growled so loud I thought they would hear me," Cota lamented.

"I get it, you were hungry!" Bear rolled his eyes and quickly realized that Cota was enjoying his new role as storyteller. *Enjoying it too much!* thought Bear.

"Everything was going like Biggs and Master wanted until the cows, for no apparent reason, darted off the trail and shot down across the brook. Master was yelling and swearing like a mad man, and Biggs ran in circles, like he didn't know what to do. Master was cursing at the cows and shouting at Biggs. Then cursing at Biggs, and shouting at the cows. It was chaos!"

"Is this when it gets crazy?" implored Bear.
"Yes!" said Cota "I was about…"
"It's about time!" Bear interrupted.

"If you would just be quiet!" Cota was fearlessly barking at Bear, not the least bit concerned that the big black mound of claws and fur could rip him into a pile of raven food in a few quick seconds. Cota scratched his ear with a hind paw, then continued.

"I raced down from the ridge top and followed them across

the brook and into the woods. It was new terrain, so I had to lay back, careful to not be spotted, and ready to bolt back the way I came. Circling around behind Master, I moved up along another bank, hidden by the thick laurels."

"At one point I was so close to Master, but he never knew I was there," Cota bragged.

"Still, I was more hungry than curious and hoped that Master would forget about the calf. But he didn't and scooped her up in his arms again. If not, I would have been eating the calf and missed all that happened next." Cota didn't want to leave out a single detail.

Bear was losing interest.

"Biggs was way ahead. I could hear him barking in the distance, so I forgot about Master and the calf, and sprinted on toward all the commotion."

"There was more barking!" Cota's voice still a raspy whisper, but rising in volume as he spoke. "Biggs was suddenly silent, and all I could hear was the deep angry snarls of two pit bulls. I was sprinting through the laurels as fast as I could, trying to catch up!"

"The barking got louder and more vicious. Still, there was not a sound from Biggs. Master was way behind and I could hear him yelling and swearing for Biggs to come back. He must have heard the pit bulls, too."

"Then what?!" Bear growled, now into the story.
"I made my way to the edge of a clearing. The angry snarls from the pit bulls was terrifying, even to me. Then I heard another human yelling, but I couldn't understand the words."
"Who was it?" asked Bear.
"Don't know. Man that lived there I guess. He came out of

an old run down cabin carrying a big gun, the one they call a 'sawed-off' I think," said Cota.

"Pit bulls his?" asked Bear.

"Suppose so. They were chained out in front of the cabin," Cota replied.

"Oh, they were on chains!" Bear said relieved. "Where was Biggs?"

"This is where the story gets crazy!" Cota's eyes were wide like he was reliving the scene all over again. "Biggs was only a few feet from them big snarly pits. He was just staring them down. Like, he was not afraid. He just stood all bowed up like he could take 'em down. I'm telling you those pit bulls would have ripped him to shreds in a second. But, Biggs just stood there and stared 'em down! Craziest thing I've ever seen!"

"That what got 'em riled up? Biggs?" Bear asked, anxious to hear more.

"No, I don't think so. It was the cows. They had plowed right through there, right in front of the cabin. I could tell by all the churned-up mud and hoof prints. It was a mess!"

"What about the man? What did he do?" asked Bear.

"Oh man, he was all tore-up! Yelling, cursing and waiving that gun around. He was the scariest human I'd ever seen!" Cota's wide eyes got wider. "He had long black hair and a long dark beard. His eyes were even darker. His muddy boots were laced up over his pants. He had drawings all over his arms and back. I'm telling you, scariest thing I've ever seen--that man and them dogs!"

"Where was Master? And Biggs? He still facing off with the pit bulls?" Bear wanted to know more.

Cota continued, "Master finally caught up. Yelling the whole way, I heard him coming and thought, this is going to be trouble. Master left the calf behind, because I couldn't see it and couldn't even hear it bawlin'. But I forgot about the calf because as soon as Master showed up, the man swung his sawed-off around and pointed it at Master's head."

"Whoa, what did he do?" Bear asked.
"Right there, I knew where Biggs got his fearless attitude!" Cota proclaimed. "Master just kept coming. Walked right up to that scary man, pointing his finger, and yelling."

Cota went on, "I just knew Master was going to get killed, and them dogs was going to eat Biggs. I was scared and didn't want to watch it all happen. I wanted to leave. But I couldn't. I was frozen stiff."

"Why didn't you do something? Why didn't you help?" Bear asked with great disapproval.

Cota snapped out of the story and barked back at Bear, "You know that if a coyote ran in the middle of all that, guns would be going off. ON ME!"

Cota scolded Bear with his eyes for asking such a question.

"Understand," Bear conceded. "Go on, finish the story."

Cota stood and shook the loose fur from his coat, like he needed to shake free of the terror unfolding. "So, the man was yelling at Master, still pointing the gun at him. I could barely understand his words, but he was mad about the cows trampling through his yard. I could make that much out. He was real mad, pointing to the ground and all the hoof prints. I'm telling you though, there was not a stitch of grass around that whole place. There was no yard, just mud. Not sure why he was all worked up."

"Some folks just like a reason to get worked up," Bear said, casually.

Cota nodded, casual too, and said, "yep, they both had reason to get worked up, it seemed. The man was mad about his torn-up yard, Master was mad about the gun in his face."

"Then it really ramped up!" Cota announced.
"Oh?" said Bear, "There's more?"
"Oh yes! A lot more!" Cota's eyes were wide again. "Told you that I was hiding in the woods just beyond the clearing. It was the middle of the day but dark back there. We were way back in the woods, and the trees hovered like nighttime, but I could see it all."

"See what?" Bear demanded.

"I could see Master and the man, and Biggs still only a few feet away from the chained-up dogs. They were going crazy, about to pull the chains right out of the ground. I'm telling you if one of them chains snapped, Biggs would have been dead in two seconds. But he didn't move." Cota was in full story-telling mode.

"It all happened so fast I almost missed it. But I saw the whole thing. The man suddenly moved his gun away from Master and pointed it at Biggs. He was raising it up, to take aim. I just knew he was going to shoot Biggs," Cota said, frantically.

"Oh man, what did Master do?" asked Bear.

"This is the part I almost missed!" said Cota. "Master pulled a gun from under his coat and off his belt so fast, and before that man had time to raise his sawed-off, Master rushed right up to the crazy man, pointing the gun at his head!"

"The pit bulls were still raging, and I couldn't hear what was said next. But, the man slowly lowered his gun, bent over, then laid it on the ground. Slowly, he backed up, then stood with his hands on his hips. He was scared, I could tell. But he was still running his mouth."

"Master didn't say much else, but walked over to Biggs. He kept the gun pointed at the man and never took his eyes off him. Still, he leaned down and found the back of Biggs's head with his other hand and grabbed him by the collar. Biggs snarled one last time at the pit bulls, then walked into the woods with Master, the same direction the cows had gone earlier."

The moment passed in silence and neither Bear, nor Cota, spoke.

Finally, Bear asked, "Did you follow them?"

"No," Cota said. "I had seen enough and wanted to get out of there. But that's not all of the story!"

Bear didn't speak, he just waited for Cota to continue.

"I trekked back into the laurels, then topped over the opposite ridge. I hadn't done anything but watch all the action, but I was worn out, like I'd been in a fight. Even forgot about being hungry, until I found the stream and lapped-up a mouthful of water. It hit my stomach hard and I suddenly needed to find something to eat."

"You're always hungry for a little thing," said Bear.
"Maybe," Cota sort of agreed. "But, you might hate me for what I thought next.
"Oh yeah?" Bear titled his head, wondering what could be next.
"I remembered that Master left that calf behind. He didn't go back for it," Cota grinned.
Bear shook his head, "you're right, but I understand. You find

it?"

"Oh yeah, I found it all right!" Cota retorted. "Soon as the thought hit me, I turned and sprinted back up the ridge, cut down through the laurels, and headed in the direction of the swamps. But I was too late."

"It was near dark by then and I couldn't understand why that little cow wasn't bawlin' her head off. I couldn't hear a thing." Cota lamented.
"Something else get to her first?" Bear knew the answer before he asked.

Cota had become quite the storyteller and didn't directly answer, he just kept telling, "I tracked around the brook we crossed earlier, and then caught her scent soon after. I picked up the pace, not sprinting, but moving fast and low. Soon as I came over the rise, there she was, laying in the field."

Cota paused, took a deep breathe, then said, "and Biggs was right there, standing guard over her!"

Bear laughed with such joy that it startled Cota right out of his story. Then Cota smiled, too.

"Yep, I know," Cota said, still smiling. "That's when I became a fan of our friend, Biggs."

Moments passed and the laughter of Cota and Bear eventually tapered off into a long sigh of silence. They sat for awhile, Cota was thinking about Biggs, wondering where he might be. Wondering how he might survive out there on his own. Then he looked at Bear and wondered how he could convince him to help look for Biggs.

He's still alive and he needs our help, Cota thought.

Cota's story reminded them both there was something special

about Biggs. But, is wasn't enough to persuade Bear that he was still alive.

"I'm going to miss him," Bear suddenly said.

As the moment simmered, Cota finished his story, "Biggs sat with that calf all night. Master found them the next morning. That was the happiest I'd ever seen a human."
"You watched them all night?" Bear noticed out loud.
Cota looked down, like he'd been caught, then said, "yeah, I circled the clearing several times. They never knew I was there, but Biggs was on alert the whole time. I climbed on a rock and watched them all night."
"Why?" asked Bear.
"Don't know for sure. But glad I did. In the hours right before light, I heard a pack of coyotes calling. It was the Northern Ridge Pack. I knew it was them because there are so many in that pack. Had not seen or heard them in many moons, but they showed up that night. Soon as I was sure where they were, I jumped off the rock sprinted up high on the ridge," said Cota.
"Why, you scared of them, too?" asked Bear.
"No!" Cota snapped back. "Let me finish. I knew that if they got much closer, they would catch scent of the calf. If they did it would be the end for her, and for Biggs," Cota retorted.
"So, why did you run on the ridge?" Bear asked.
"I ran up there to be heard!" Cota said defiantly. "I ran all the way to the top of the ridge, then howled into the darkness."
"What did you say?" Bear sort of knew already, but had to ask.
"I started in rapid-fire yipping, then rolled into a blood piercing squeal, followed by three long, deep barks. Then did it all over, three more times. My lone howls rolled through the valley, then echoed off the distant ridge. Soon, the Northern Pack replied. They heard my dire warning of danger, and knew not to come any closer. They heeded my friendly plea and left."

"After a long silence, I heard the leader of the Pack bellow out one last howl. He was thanking me. They were further away, moving north," Cota said, still relieved.

"You saved Biggs and the calf," Bear smiled.

"Yeah, suppose I did," Cota replied. "And, I haven't let another pack of coyotes attack on Biggs's place since."

Neither Biggs nor Cota said another word for what remained of the night. Bear ambled around the trees, then found a spot to lay on the forest floor. Cota curled up and lay atop the moss-covered rock. Neither of them slept.

Joe Cundiff

30

BETRAYED

The sound of human voices awoke Cota from his nap. It was late afternoon, and the sun was warm. Bear was long gone, or so Cota thought. He had slipped away without a word after their talk the night before. Cota was not concerned with Bear at the moment. The voices, and the steps of the humans crunching leaves were getting closer. Dangerously close!

Cota knew he needed to run. *Which way?* He thought in a panic. Still not sure which direction they were coming, he lay still as a rock. Cota's ears perked straight-up and twitched to gather every flicker of sound.

The sudden growl from behind was soft and low, but startled him even more! Cota slowly rolled his head around and saw Bear.

"This way," was all he said.

Cota rose to a crouch and followed Bear. Together, they slipped off into the pines, treading quietly on the blanket of needles. Neither uttered a sound until safely away from the hunters.

"What were they after?" Cota whispered, breaking the silence.
"Bird hunters, I think," replied Bear.
"Chasing the ruffed grouse up here in the high country," Cota said, relieved they were not after him, but knowing that given the chance, a hunter would take any shot at a coyote.
"Yep, but soon the snowfall will be too deep for the humans to get up here," Bear replied.
"I'll winter in these pines, safer up here. If I can find enough to

19

eat," said Cota.

"I will burrow further up, in The Cliffs," said Bear.

The Cliffs, thought Cota.

Hearing the words took him back to a darker time. A time he felt most betrayed.

"What's wrong?" Bear could see the look of despair on Cota's face.

Cota was staring blankly into the woods. He had no idea that his expression suddenly revealed all the angst pent-up inside of him. Cota's mind flashed back to The Cliffs, and his body slunk, desperate to forget the betrayal.

"I'll tell you tonight," Cota said, deflecting the question. "Meet me in the woods again?"

"He won't be there you know," Bear said, reminding Cota that he believed Biggs was dead.

Cota would not concede. "Maybe not, but meet me there anyway."

"Same place." It was more a statement than a question from Bear.

"Yep," Cota said as he turned and walked away. "Same place."

***

A steep ridge dropped down to the small patch of woods that was a hundred feet or so from the Barn. From there they could see across the open field, toward the sacred circle of dirt, where Biggs once reigned. But, the big square doghouse was long gone, swept into the sky by the wind funnel, and the clamor of chain links that once rolled rhythmically across the ground, lay eerily silent in the dirt.

Biggs was gone, but his presence remained thick as wet fog

hanging in the night air.

Cota was there, pacing in a semi-circle, when Bear finally arrived. He didn't stop to look at Bear but burst out with all that was on his mind.

"You said you're going to winter in The Cliffs," Cota said.
"Yes, why?" Bear asked, undeterred by the abruptness.
"Unless you plan to sleep all winter, you won't like it up there."
"I like it fine up there," Cota snorted, ignoring the fact that he did not plan to winter in The Cliffs.
"I went to The Cliffs after Master tried to kill me."
"Ah, I see," said Bear as he circled the boulder where Cota was normally perched.
"I stayed up there for days. Alone," Cota continued. "I didn't want to see, or talk to another soul. Especially not Biggs."

Bear circled the boulder again, while Cota continued pacing. The coyote was more worked up than ever, so Bear found a soft spot and laid down. Bear tried to look his friend in the eyes, but Cota's attention was scattered.

Cota paced back-and-forth in a short rapid burst. He would dart one direction, then suddenly twitch his head back the other direction, swiveling on hind legs while his front paws never seemed to leave the ground. Back-and-forth, back-and-forth! Bear's eyes followed in rhythm as he waited and listened.

Cota's words rambled on more rapid than his frantic pacing.

"I mean, Master tried to kill me. I had not hurt him, and Biggs was my friend. I was no threat, so why did he try to kill me?"

Bear raised his head and took a breath, but before he could speak, Cota fired-off more questions.

"Do you think Biggs set me up? I mean, it seems like maybe he did. How did Master know I would be there?" Cota stopped pacing and finally looked Bear in the eyes. Bear tilted his head and gave Cota a patronizing grin. Cota was annoyed by Bear's haughty demeanor, but he was too worked-up to quit.

"Biggs wouldn't do that! Would he?" Cota's voice was losing conviction.

Bear started to answer, but Cota wasn't done. Bear listened until Cota rambled out of questions.

"I don't think Biggs would set me up. So, why do I feel bad about leaving? I just walked away and never talked to him again. Now he's gone!"
"So, that's what this is about," said Bear.
"About what?" Cota was more confused. "This is about what?"
"You feel guilty," said Bear, his eyes piercing into Cota's.

His words stung like a dozen hornet stings.

"Why should I feel guilty? Master tried to kill me!" Cota had been too busy being offended and feeling betrayed to ever consider feeling guilty. Yet, Bear's words and his powerful presence made him stop and think. "Why do you think I feel guilty?"
"Because you won't accept that he is gone. That's why you want him to still be alive." Bear's words cut even deeper.
"That's not true! I mean--I do still want him to be alive. I mean--I believe he is still alive, but I don't feel guilty. That's not it!" Cota looked hard at Bear. "Why don't you believe me?"

Bear let the moment simmer but didn't let up. "Because there is no way he could have survived that wind storm. And, you have no proof that he is alive. He's gone, and you need to let it go."

Cota walked over to the moss-covered boulder but was too mad to climb on top. Dejected, he just sat down in the dirt and would not look at Bear.

Bear knew his words hurt, but he felt Cota needed to face the truth. Biggs was gone, likely dead.

"It's time to move on." He tried to say it gently.
"If you think he is dead, then why do you come here each night?" asked Cota.
Bear grinned at Cota's cutting jab, then his face turned sour, "I miss him, too."

Bear's booming words fell like a curtain call, a painful finale.

"I can't move on until I know for sure. I need to know what happened."
"Why?" Bear demanded.

Cota turned, faced Bear, and looked him in the eyes again.

"Because he came looking for me."

They both looked away, toward the Barn, then Cota continued.

"Several nights after The Shot, Biggs went into The Grove and challenged The Sadie Hollow Pack to find out if they knew where I went. They could have easily killed him. That was either really brave or really dumb of Biggs."

"How do you know all of this? I thought you went to The Cliffs?" Bear asked.

"I did. But that night I heard Biggs call out to the Pack. It was quiet and the winds were still, right before the rain. I know Biggs must have been out there, on the ridge of The Saddle, waiting for that exact moment. The winds always lay calm, right before the skies erupt. Biggs knew it and he waited. He knew I would hear it too. The brutal sounds of his lone howl still ring in my ears. I can't make the ringing stop. I heard him from all the way up there," Cota rolled his head. "I heard him from The Cliffs."

Bear didn't speak.

"I had to know why, so I was already in The Grove when The Sadie Hollow Pack led Biggs back, into their inner chambers. I heard it all."
"Why did Biggs want to find you?" Bear asked.

"I didn't know why at the time. I was still so mad and didn't really care. I didn't understand until after he went missing. It's my fault he left. That's why I have to find him," said Cota.
"The wind funnel swept him away. He's dead. That is not your fault!"
"I don't believe that! I don't believe he is dead." Cota jumped up on the boulder and stared down at Bear.

"That first morning in the Bowl, after the fight with the bloodhounds, I tried to get him to come run with me. I wanted him to know what it was like to be free. I didn't understand his life. I didn't know he had a purpose. I thought my way was better. I didn't understand why he would go back and be bound to that chain. I kept trying to get him to run with me."
"You can blame yourself, but that won't bring him back," said Bear.
"You just don't get it! The morning after the council in The Grove, that's when the Farmer shot one of The Sadie Hollow Pack," Cota lamented.
"I remember," said Bear.

"Biggs rode up in the back of Master's truck. I'll never forget the look on his face. It was so much pain. Master and the Farmer, they were laughing and celebrating. Biggs was in so much pain. A part of Biggs died with that coyote. I could see it in his eyes."

"Then what happened?" asked Bear.

"Master was calling Biggs to come. But, he didn't move. Not for a long time. Finally, Biggs jumped out of the truck, turned away, and ran back toward the Farm. I watched until he disappeared across the field, then I headed back to The Cliffs."

Cota took a deep breath, then said, "I could see it all from up there."

"See what?"

"I watched the wind funnel rip through the valley. I knew it went straight through the Farm. It all happened so fast. By the time I got back down, it was all over. The top of the Barn was ripped off, trees broken in half, and stuff was everywhere. And, Biggs was gone."

Bear didn't press Cota any further. They both sat quietly, listening to the endless sounds of nighttime.

In the distance, the blaring of a train horn preceded the rumble of iron stallions rolling through the darkness.

Rain fell from the sky.

Joe Cundiff

31

MASTER'S SHADOW

The days became weeks, and soon the hours passed in random. Still, no sign of Biggs. Not a single clue. Bear ended his nightly ritual of sitting with Cota in the woods near the Barn. Winter was coming soon, and Bear ventured out to forage for food. He only had a few more weeks to fatten up before heading to The Cliffs for a long winter's nap.

Cota though, was committed to his belief that Biggs was out there, and still alive. He had no evidence, as Bear had so often pointed out, but Cota was not ready to give up. Not yet.

"I'm glad Bear is gone," Cota said out loud. "I'm tired of trying to make him believe."

"I will find Biggs."

Cota's only ally was not one he could confide in. Master was still looking for Biggs, and Cota was watching him closely. For days and weeks after Biggs went missing, Master searched every patch and every corner of the Farm, and beyond. And Cota was there, in the shadows, watching him.

Cota knew Master was looking for Biggs. It was much different when he searched for a momma cow and a new calf. She would be in the lowlands, curled up in a soft patch near the water with her baby. He had seen it all dozens of times. But, Cota trailed Master each day, as he stumbled up every ridge and tracked every fence line.

The third time Master fell, he tumbled down a steep ridge and rolled to a stop, colliding with an oak tree. Cota watched as Master gripped his knee and winced in pain. He wanted to hate Master, but he was worried. Cota wanted to help, but there was nothing he could do. The coyote remained hidden in the brush, weary of the black-handle gun strapped to Master's belt.

Cota didn't think Master was going to get up, but finally he rolled over, grabbed the tree, and pulled himself up to his feet. The man's face was agony. In frustration, he yelled out once more for his dog. "BIGGS! Where are ya, Boyha?!" It was a different kind of yell. Cota thought Master was mad at Biggs, blaming his lost dog for the fall.

Master staggered and limped the entire painful walk back to the barn.
"If Master believed Biggs was dead, he would quit looking." Cota spoke from the perch of his rock like Bear was still there listening.

Cota returned alone every night to the same patch of woods, usually before Master went home. Each night, Master would walk over where Biggs's dog house once stood. Cota watched as he would bend down to pick up the links of chain laying on the ground. He studied it carefully, as if the answer would suddenly reveal itself from the cold metal.

"Where are you boy?" Master spoke into the wind, hoping his words would sail through the night and land on the ears of his beloved dog. "I know you're out there."

The windless night was so calm that a lone falcon feather teetered on a branch above Cota's head but did not fall. He could smell it though. Cota knew the majestic bird was long gone, likely nesting in the Cliffs.

Cota could also smell the despair in Master's lingering words.

Master let loose of his hold on the chain, and the clamor of collapsing links echoed through the Barn and across the Bluestone River. A painful reminder of all that was missing. The sounds of dancing metal across the barren ground was a memory slowly fading away.

"I believe you," Cota whispered. His raspy voice sullen but filled with hope.

Hours after Master had left, Cota was still perched atop his boulder, keeping watch over the Barn. It had become his nightly ritual. Bear had warned Cota that he needed to end his obsession.

"Biggs is not coming back!" Bear had demanded.

But Cota really didn't have anywhere else to be, or anything else to do. He knew that after Master left, there would be no humans around the Barn, so Cota could camp safely in the woods.

Cota stood atop the rock, stretched his legs long and arched his back high, then shook the dew from his fur coat. Master was obsessed with the Chain, and Cota wanted to find out why.

The night was clear, and the sky was filled with stars. A quarter moon floated at an angle on the eastern edge of the dome. The moon shed little light, but Cota was too cautious to traipse across the open field. Instead, he followed his normal route through the woods and down to the river. From there, Cota skirted along the banks, safely out of sight.
There were three rabbits, a groundhog, and dozens of field mice feeding on the clover and grass in the field. Cota could not see them, but a subtle draft of wind swirled the world of nightly news across the field, over the river bank, and down toward Cota's upturned snout. He stopped for a moment and inhaled all the elements.

There was plenty to eat in the field, but Cota was on a mission. He wanted to inspect Biggs's chain one more time. Master studied it every night, and Cota wanted to know why.

There were no lights at the Barn, so Cota walked freely about. He knew that no one was around, but the scent of human, mostly all of it Master, was wreaking havoc on Cota's senses. He pressed on and circled the Barn.

The scent of Biggs remained too, but it was barely detectable. Cota walked across the sacred circle of dirt and stopped at the Chain.

"What is Master trying to find?"

Cota walked around the chain, then stepped across it,

before turning a full circle in one spot. He sat down and stared at the end of the chain. Slowly, his eyes traced along each link back toward the center, where his eyes met the jumbled heap of barbed wire and chain wrapped in a tangled mess.

"Master has been looking at the wrong end," he said out loud.

Cota stood and walked over the heap of wire and metal, wrapped around the old wheel axle.

Biggs was trying to get free.

Cota sat down in the center of the sacred circle and closed his eyes. Suddenly, the night of the great wind funnel flashed through his mind. He imagined being there with Biggs as the wind swirled chaos around them. Violent gusts shredding trees and ripping the roof off the Barn.

Biggs would have been frantic. Why didn't he dart across the center, like he always had, and break free? Cota had seen Biggs break loose many times. He could see it all happening in his mind. But then he looked back at the center of the circle.

The chain was tangled-up in the wire. He couldn't break free!

Cota walked back toward the end of the links, leaned down and grabbed the chain with his teeth. Slowly, he raised it in the air and stood tall. The weight was surprising, and he gripped tighter in his mouth to keep it from slipping. *How did Biggs live connected to this chain?*

Cota lowered his head and felt the weight drop, then opened and closed his mouth quickly, gaining a better grip on the chain. Again, he raised his head and heard the familiar roll of links lifting off the ground. The weight and balance of the chain steadied in his grip. Cota pulled until all the links extended into the air.

Cota's legs quivered as his claws gripped the hard ground. He struggled to keep the chain taut, and his admiration for Biggs grew stronger.

This chain is much heavier than I thought. Biggs made this look easy.

With his mouth clamped firmly around the chain, Cota tried to run. But, he didn't make it three steps before the links twisted into one solid torqued piece of iron and ripped painfully from his teeth. The jolt flipped him around, but he managed to stay on his feet. Stunned, he stood and looked at the heap of metal laying on the ground. Blood dripped from his mouth.

With his eyes, Cota followed each link back to the center of the circle. He had seen Biggs run thousands of laps around his sacred patch of dirt. The rhythm kept pace with his prance, and the chain spun fluidly on the wheel axle, as if it were part of Biggs's being.

Cota suddenly realized what happened and his eyes filled with tears. Tears of pain and tears filled with the joy of discovery. Cota burst from the circle and scampered toward the Barn. The old oil drum stood next to the side wall on the corner near the door. Cota raised up on his hind haunches and landed his front paws on the rim of the drum. It was still there where Master had left it. Cota carefully clamped his teeth around the twisted chain link, pushed away from the drum, and walked back to Biggs's circle of dirt.

Cota sat down and dropped the single link next to the rest of the chain, and then studied it all curiously.

"Biggs was running in circles trying to get free. That's what broke the chain!"

Cota figured it out, then stood tall and looked out into the woods. Turning slowly, his eyes scanned across the open field. Peering beyond the river and his eyes locked on the glaring beam of light piercing the darkness and flickering through dancing branches.

The train's horn roared above the rumble of tracks, speaking once more to Cota. This time he knew.

"Biggs is out there!"

***

By the time the sun lifted across the eastern rim, Cota's coat had dried from his swim across the river. He was miles away from the Farm, walking along the railroad tracks. The powerful scent of diesel fuel and creosote was strong. If Biggs had traveled this route, Cota would never pick up the trail. Still, Cota believed he was on the right track, so he kept going.

Through the darkness of night, Cota traveled freely and undetected. But the daylight created challenges, especially as he traipsed near human activity. Of course, he had plenty of time to jump off the tracks and hide when the trains rolled past. But the tracks were leading him to the nearest town, and a mix of human scent was swirling in the air.

The town was within sight, but he knew better than to go near. At least not out in the open. So, Cota abandoned the tracks and headed for the woods where he would skirt around, and hopefully pick up the tracks again.

It was mid-morning and Cota was tired. He found a stream in the woods and lapped up as much water as he could hold. The sun was warm and suddenly the fatigue hit his legs like a falling tree. Cota found a safe place in the moss-covered rocks, curled up, and went to sleep.

***

Train horns, car horns, crossing bars rising and falling with lights flashing and bells ringing. Cota slept through it all. He was in a deep trance of sleep, seemingly lost to the world around him. But his ears never slept, and the gateway to his brain was on constant alert. Cota was hidden safely in the woods, but he had never been this close to a town. Surprisingly, the chaos and clamor only lulled him deeper into his slumber.

But the subtle click-clank of metal sliding across metal sent shock waves through his radar-like ears, and in less than an instant, Cota was wide-awake. His insides raged with the turmoil of impending danger, but his body did not move. Cota did not panic.

The sounds of a bolt-action rifle sliding a bullet into the chamber screamed through his subconscious. Cota's eyes scanned an unfamiliar scene, his ears on high alert. Then he heard it again, only it was more scrape-clank follow by scrape-slide-clank. Then CLANK CLANK CLANK!

Cota's eyes locked on the man, but he did not move. He didn't run or even duck. Peering through the woods, Cota could see the man standing outside, behind the diner. He was not loading a gun, or even holding a gun. The sounds that shocked Cota awake were the scraping of gravy from a metal pan with a big metal spoon.

Cota began to breathe again. Soon his heart would find its normal rhythm. He closed his eyes and tried to go back to sleep, but the draft of turkey gravy and baked beans would not allow it. Cota's stomach churned painfully and growled with an angry hunger.

Soon Cota was on his feet and moving silently through the woods, getting closer to the diner with each step. He had never smelled such a mixture of flavors, and it was dangerously intoxicating. Cota had not eaten in days. Until that moment, he had not even thought about eating, which had never happened before.

Worrying about Biggs had consumed the coyote. But now, his aching stomach took control of his mind and body.

"How can I get to that barrel?"

Cota stood at the edge of the woods, concealed by the overgrowth of kudzu vines crawling into the trees. Only his nose and eyes appeared from the brush. He studied the scene closely, searching for an angle to get to the food. There wasn't one. At least not one that he could survive.

"I'll wait here until dark," Cota concluded.

But he continued to study the scene and surroundings, taking in all the sights and unfamiliar sounds of town life. *I'll bet no other coyote has seen all of this,* he thought proudly. *At least not this close.*

Cota's stomach ached more with each passing minute, but he was content to wait until dark. Especially each time he saw the man scrape more food into the barrel.

"That will last me a week, if I can get there without getting killed," Cota whispered, as if someone might be listening.

Then he forgot all about being hungry. Cota could not believe his eyes.

"Master's truck! What is he doing here?" The truck was parked on the side road, near the diner.

Cota stared intently across the tracks and through the alley at the back door of the diner.
While Master was inside, Cota would have given anything to know what was happening inside the diner, but he could only hide in the kudzu and wonder.

Master sat on a stool at the counter and ordered a bowl of beans and cornbread. The waitress mumbled to herself as she wrote, then ripped the sheet from her pad and passed it into the kitchen. In one fluid motion she grabbed the handle to the coffee pot, spun, and filled Master's mug. She was in the middle of a conversation with the folks three stools down and loudly resumed telling her story, while spilling coffee.

"That big dog was the scariest thing I've ever seen in this town. He must have belonged to someone, had three-feet of broken chain dangling from his collar."

Master spit his coffee back across the mug and stood facing the waitress.

"What kind of dog was it?
"Um, not sure. German Shepherd, I think."
"Which way?"
"Which way, what?"
"WHICH WAY DID MY DOG GO?"

Suddenly appalled that anyone would claim that beast, the waitress was speechless and could not hide her distasteful expression.

"WHICH WAY?!"

Slowly, she raised her arm, pointing toward the tracks.
"Escaped the police and headed that way. They tried to shoot him but missed," she announced to the whole diner.

Master winced at the thought of someone shooting at Biggs, then he ran through the kitchen without asking and burst out the back door.

"Master!" Cota barked loudly.

Cota's eyes traced every step as Master charged down the alleyway and headed for the tracks. Cota forgot about hiding and took off after him.

What are you after? Cota wondered, as he skirted along the edge of the woods behind the town.

Master quickly left his truck and the town behind. Cota followed along, more brazen in his appearance the further he traipsed after Master. Still, instincts prevailed, and he wove in and out of the trees, keeping out of sight as much as he could. Cota had no idea where Master was going, but he would not let him go alone. Cota could tell, it was more than mere curiosity. Master was on a mission.

He knows something about Biggs!

Hours passed and Master's tired, worn boots scuffed along the wooden ties as he walked between the rails. His pace became slower and his voice waned with despair. Cota had no idea what happened in the diner, but based upon Master's reaction, he knew it had to do with Biggs. Master walked in earnest, desperately calling for his dog.

"BIGGS! Come home, boyah!"

Cota was thrilled and tormented by each outburst. He trailed Master the whole way, mostly skirting the edge of the woods, not once gathering the slightest hint of Biggs's scent. Still, he had hope.

Both darkness and the temperature fell suddenly in the late Appalachian autumn. Master stopped on the railroad

tracks and faced the woods. Cota moved undetected
closer to the tracks where he watched and listened.
Master looked up into the sky, then down at his boots.
Master was tired and getting cold. He had not come
prepared to search through the night, and it was time to
turn back.

Cota could feel the despair, dripping from Master's face.

It would be a long walk in the dark back to his truck.
Biggs was out there somewhere, but long gone. Dejected,
Master turned and began the painful journey, retracing
each step along the train tracks back to town.

Cota was right next to the tracks and ducked into the
brush. Master scuffed by, merely a few feet away. The
scent of sweat and despair was overwhelming. As soon
as Master passed, Cota climbed up the bank and stood in
the center of the tracks. The image of Master faded
slowly into the darkness. The coyote sat down and
listened until the echo of scuffing leather grew silent.

The rush of water cascading across rocks interrupted the
night, and stole Cota's attention. While tracking Master,
Cota had not stopped once for drink. The sweet sounds
of the stream was calling, so Cota stood and turned away
from the town, walking along the tracks toward the sound
of rushing water.

Cota scampered down off the tracks. He had no idea that
weeks earlier, Biggs had followed those same railroad
tracks as he ran from the town, with three feet of chain
dangling from his collar. Cota never picked up the scent
because he had followed Master from the woods, and the

scent was impossible to trace on the railroad. But when Cota left the tracks and headed for the stream, it hit him.

"Biggs!"

The same rush of water had captured Biggs's worn and tired attention. Cota picked up the scent as soon as he dropped down off the high bank of the railroad tracks and into the woods.

"Biggs was here!"

Cota turned and quickly ran back up the tracks. He wanted so desperately to run and tell Master. But he knew he could not. The joy and despair was a brutal mix. Hope prevailed, and Cota stood tall on his hind haunches and bellowed his findings into the night.

The lone howl was piercing and pleaful.

Master stopped along the tracks as the echo of a coyote's howl lingered. He didn't turn around, but peered sharply across his right shoulder. There was only darkness and the unknown. The concerned scowl he'd worn all afternoon was swept away by the subtle smile spreading across his face.

"Better not let my Biggs hear you!"

The irony of Master's warning fell softly into the darkness as he continued on his journey back to his truck, and back home. Cota stood alone on the tracks with only one desire. That Biggs would hear his plea and respond.

Cota waited, hopeful, but knowing Biggs would not reply. But Cota knew without a doubt that Biggs was out there.

The lone coyote scoured the ground with his snout until he picked up the scent again. Cota raised his head high into the air and bellowed out another howl.

"I'm coming Biggs, I'm coming to get you."

Joe Cundiff

32

THE RIVER'S END

The silence of such bitter cold is deafening. So many shades of white, shifting into subtle grays, and hues undefined. Parched air devoid of life, floating breathless and lingering in time. Cota had no fear of the elements, but rather embraced each moment, leaning into life as if he owned them all. It was what he admired most about Biggs. The fearless spirit that had defined him, and set him free.

Standing tall atop the highest mountain, a place called Archibald Peaks, the world below and beyond appeared vast and barren, yet Cota laid claim to the moment. A moment sublime, etched in the frozen chambers of Cota's soul. A moment already gone too soon.

It was too cold even to snow. As the arctic wind bellowing from the north ripped across Cota's face and back, his fur brittled with ice. Cota peered into space, his body sculpted and carved away by the hard months of winter. It was the longest stretch of cold he could recall. His worried face was glazed with crystals of ice. A snowy beard etched and woven into to his fur. Long whiskers wrapped in frozen moisture drooped from his snout. Yet, his eyes still glowed deep and golden, undaunted by the vast expanse of frozen tundra surrounding him. From his perch, Cota could see hundreds of miles in all directions. Appalachian mountain tops, carved by the great waters of time, all covered in an endless glaze of white. From Cota's view, the entire world was buried in the wrath of winter, and locked in silence.

Cota stood defiant to it all--the harsh elements, time, and the unknown. Staring into the face of the wind and biting cold,

Cota's life on the run found purpose.

"I know you're out there Biggs, and I will find you."

The minutes slowly turned past hours, and the last glimmer of light slowly drifted west, in search of another day. Cota stayed on guard all night.

"Biggs never slept in his house," Cota spoke to the world, but no one was listening.

There was not another set of ears within miles, and the air was so cold it felt like the world would end. But Cota knew that Biggs was out there, and he was worried about his friend. The German shepherd was tough and could handle the cold. Cota knew Biggs could survive the elements, but neither he nor Biggs had ever experienced this much snow and such bitter cold in one winter. Biggs was out there, hidden in the maze of mountains and ridges that stretched deep into the darkness.

Cota's claws dug into the ice-covered rocks, and his legs locked in a solid stance. He inhaled the brutally thin air, nearly freezing his lungs. He had a message to send, and from atop the highest peak, Cota bellowed from the depths of his despair. A resounding high-pitched howl of anguish and wanting that charged the night with the currency of freedom.

At that very moment, as Cota cried out in a soulful plea from the peak of the highest mountain, Biggs was all alone, and trembling with fear. Biggs was hidden within the confines of an old Shack, being stalked by a hungry mountain lion.

Biggs would not hear Cota's cry, but the lingering vibration of the lone howl sailed softly above. Held within the wake that followed, a gentle wave of air fell from the sky, landing atop the snow-covered beams of the Shack. What remained was less than a whisper, yet held the power to shift a mound of snow down onto the back of a mountain lion, sending the big cat scampering into the night. And saving Biggs from certain death.

***

It had been months since the day Cota followed Master along the railroad tracks from the diner, and he was still searching. That day Cota had traced Biggs's scent into the woods, but he lost it as soon as he reached the sulphur-filled stream. The stench rising from the black water, contaminated by the mines, was too strong. He never picked up the scent again. But knowing that Biggs was alive was all that mattered.

Cota would not quit looking until he found his friend.

With each day that passed, Cota felt more guilt. He needed to find Biggs. He wanted to make things right again. He needed to bring Biggs home.

***

After the last snow had fallen, and the days became longer, the sun once again filled the sky. Cota knew the warm months were fast approaching, and Bear would soon emerge from his winter den.

"Bear will believe me now, and he'll know what to do."

Poised with confidence and the hope he could find Bear, Cota began the long journey back to The Cliffs. It would take weeks, or longer to get back, but Bear needed to know.

"The scent of Biggs will be gone, but I'll take Bear to that spot. He will have to believe me. Together we'll find him."

***

A month after he decided to find Bear, Cota was still walking. Traveling mostly at night, Cota followed the train tracks and avoided the humans. He found plenty to eat along the way but was seldom hungry. Cota lost his appetite the day Biggs disappeared. He ate only enough to survive, and it showed. Cota's thick, matted coat draped across his long thin body like a dirty rug. But he walked with purpose and often stepped it up into a gallop, urgent to share his news with Bear.

"I hope Bear believes me."

Cota ran across the long railroad trestle. He remembered crossing the bridge from the other direction, several months prior. It was the longest and highest bridge Cota had ever crossed, and he knew if he didn't make it to the other side before a train came, it would be certain death. The river was two-hundred feet or more below.

There were no vibrations rumbling the tracks beneath his feet, so he ventured on. Cota knew the trains were coming long before the familiar sounds could be heard. About mid-way, he felt safe enough to stop and look down from either side. The wind sifted through his shedding fur coat, lifting bundles of hair for the long journey down to the river. Cota raised his snout and breathed in the air. He was missing something. There was a message in the air, but he couldn't quite capture it.

What he would never know was that Biggs never made it across that bridge. He was almost to the mid-point where Cota now stood, when he had to turn and run back. Biggs barely outraced the oncoming train, and just made it close enough to leap down into the snow. Biggs never climbed back up to the bridge. Instead, he took the snow-covered road north.

The subtle swoon of spring wafted by, and Cota sensed something was awry. He would never know that his long search throughout the winter had taken him further away from

Biggs each day. He never had a chance of finding his friend. But, he was out there looking.

Cota had spent the entire winter searching for Biggs.

***

The sounds of the Town were unmistakable, and Cota knew he was getting near. It was early morning, and the sun had not yet lifted over the eastern rim, but it was too light for a ragged coyote to traipse along the tracks at the edge of town. Cota knew as much.

He had been walking all night, and his feet worn from miles of gravel and wood. Walking, or running along the tracks was awkward at best, and mostly uncomfortable. But, Cota knew it was his fastest route. The railroad tracks would lead him straight to the Farm. From there, Cota could cut through the woods and head for The Cliffs, in search of Bear.

But first he would have to get around the Town.

The crack of the rifle blast was unmistakable. It had been more than a year since Cota heard such a snap, but his body reacted in tune.

"He might not miss the next time."

Cota knew that if he heard the rifle blast, the lead bullet of death had already passed. The shot had sailed over his head, and Cota never heard the lead hit the ground. He didn't wait around for the second attempt on his life and disappeared into the woods.

Cota had been wandering in the wild for so long, he had nearly forgotten the fear of humans he learned while living in farmland. That changed in an instant, and he decided to hide in the woods until dark.

"I'll go find Bear tonight."

Cota ventured deep into the forest, then climbed the highest ridge outside of the Town. The air was cool, and he found a warm patch in the leaves to lay down. He should have been more rattled by the shot, but Cota didn't give it another thought. He slept through the entire day.

The sun had just set when he awoke. Cota stood and walked out from between the rocks. He stopped, arched his back high and stood tall on his worn paws, then shook mounds of shedding fur from his coat. He walked slowly from beneath the cloud of fur, his yellow eyes trying to focus behind squinting brows. From his perch, Cota peered beyond the darkness. Below, the Town was aglow in a random chorus of lights.

"I'm not going back down there."

Cota sat for a moment and absorbed the scene. He knew that behind each flickering light there were so many humans going about their lives. It all smelled of danger. Even in the dark, Cota thought it best to avoid going anywhere near the Town. His eyes now wide and acclimated to the dark, he turned and started walking along the ridge top, away from the Town.

It was all new terrain, but his intuition had brought him all the way from the Archibald Peaks, back to the Town. He was certain to find his way back to the Farm. Roaming through the woods felt more like home to Cota, and he was glad to be away from the railroad. The thought of telling Bear his news had revived Cota's appetite. He caught plenty to eat, gained a little weight, and felt strong.

Still, Cota's coat hung loosely across his narrow frame, his face was pointed and sharp. He walked with a bit of a gimp, his paws cracked and worn from miles on the run. The jaunt through the woods in the frigid night fueled his sense of hope. Following his innate radar, Cota soon found himself at the edge of the Farm. Cota took a deep breath, and sighed with the relief of being home. It was not his home, but he sat in the distance and admired the Farm he had grown to love.

It had been nine months since Cota had last seen the Barn. He figured it was probably safe but wanted to be sure. The coyote focused on every sight and sound for more than an hour. Nothing moved anywhere around the Barn.

"Biggs is not there."

Deep down Cota knew that it was not likely that Biggs had returned, but he still had hope. He had hoped to look down and see the image of a German shepherd, standing guard against all that roamed in the night, and to hear the echo of chain links rolling across the sacred dirt. But there was only silence. Not even a flicker of a shadow moving around the Barn.

There was no need to wait until the light of morning to confirm his findings. Cota knew Biggs was not there, so he turned and headed for The Cliffs.

"I have to find Bear."

***

Bear looked down at Cota in disbelief. Bear didn't speak, but his face spoke volumes. The frail and battered figure of a coyote standing before him was almost unrecognizable. Cota's fur was not the usual thick winter coat of a healthy coyote, but was worn with deep patches shed nearly to the skin. Bear knew it was more than just wear. Cota was malnourished and it showed. *He's aged many years in one winter,* thought Bear.

Bear wanted to admire his conviction, but it was apparent Cota had become obsessed with finding a dead dog.

"Where have you been?" Bear asked.
"From here to the Peaks and back. Looking for Biggs."

Bear knew Cota was referring to the Archibald Peaks. And he knew Cota's obsession was not healthy. Bear didn't speak, but looked away and sat down. He didn't know what to say.

"I found him!" Cota barked.
Bear's head snapped around, "What?! Where?"
"I didn't exactly find him, but I picked up his scent."
"Oh, I see," Bear was not amused.
"You don't believe me?"

Bear was a still a little groggy from his winter nap, but he knew he needed to tread lightly. Cota had spent the entire winter searching for Biggs, only to return looking like walking death. He wanted to believe Cota, but the facts could not be ignored.

"So, where is he?"
"I don't know. But he is out there."
"You searched from here to the Peaks, but didn't find him?"
Bear was examining Cota's coat as he spoke.
Noticing Bear's disdainful inspection, he snapped back, "You don't look so great either."
"I've been sleeping in a hole all winter."
"I haven't slept much."
"It shows. You need to find something to eat."
"Yeah, I suppose."
Bear stood and started walking toward the ridgeline leading down to the fields. "Come on."
"Where?" Cota asked.
"Let's find some food."

***

It took Cota the better part of two days to convince Bear that Biggs might still be alive.

"You have to believe me. I know it was him," Cota said as they talked in the patch of woods looking over the Barn. "How can you be sure? It could have been any dog." Bear knew Cota's senses were as keen as any, but he feared that Cota would believe any scent was Biggs.

"I know you don't believe me, but why did Master run out of that diner so fast and search down the tracks 'til past dark?" Cota had told Bear the story several times. "Tell me why he would do that? I'll tell you *why*. Someone in there saw Biggs, and Master went looking for him."

Bear nodded, acknowledging Cota's point but thought a long time before he replied. His words cut deep.

"Why did Master quit looking?"
"I don't know," Cota barked back. "But I know this: Biggs is out there and he needs our help. You owe me that much."
"I don't owe you…"
"You owe Biggs!" Cota fired back. "You owe it to Biggs to at least try. Biggs broke free of the chain that night and raced into the Bowl to help you. He almost *died* trying to help you. The bloodhounds would have killed him!" Cota's words tapered off. He did not need to remind Bear that he had saved Biggs from the Redbone.

Bear remained silent for a long while, letting Cota's words sink in. Bear closed his eyes and could see the look of pride on Biggs's face as he raced past that night on his way to the Bowl to fight the pack of bloodhounds.

"You're right; he didn't have to do that," Bear finally said. "Then you'll come with me?" Cota quickly stood on all four

51

ready to go.

"Yes, I'll go."

***

Cota led the way, as they walked through the night. It was an odd pairing, even for the wilds of Appalachia. A coyote and a bear traipsing together through the night. Cota was leading Bear through the woods, away from the Town and clear of the trains, to the spot where he knew Biggs had been.

They would have made it before light, if not for the charging pack of bloodhounds. The hounds were less than a hundred yards away when they picked up Bear's scent. The high-pitched yelping screeched through the air, disrupting an otherwise serene night.

"Coon hunters?" Cota asked
"Bear hunters now. They're coming for me."
"What are we going to do?" Cota asked frantically. "They're closing fast!"
"They're not after you. Do what you want. I'll lead them back to the river, then swim across. Water is up from all the snow melt. They won't make it across. They won't even try."
"Ok, I'll meet you…" Cota tried to make a plan, but Bear was already gone.

Cota darted off into the brush. He did not fear the bloodhounds but knew humans with guns would be along soon after. The high-pitched yelp and howls of a pack of hounds raced past him in the dark. Cota could not believe his ears, and clawed at the ground in disgust. He finally had Bear's help, and now he was all alone, again.

Cota hid in the brush until the hunters and their bouncing lights filtered past him and out of sight. While waiting, he thought about what Bear would do next.

"He won't come back across the river. Not tonight," Cota thought out loud.

Saying the words made it real. Cota knew Bear would not take the chance of coming back until the hunters were long gone.

"He might not come back at all," Cota lamented.

Cota's frustration boiled over, so he got up and followed the trail of hounds and hunters to the river. As Bear predicted, he led them to the riverbank, but they had no chance to make it across the swift waters. Bear was long gone. Cota watched as the hunters gathered up the raucous pack and headed back to their trucks, parked somewhere upstream, he figured.

Cota sat and gathered his bearings. The Farm was on the opposite side of the river, miles upstream. He didn't know what to do, so he did nothing. Sitting for hours staring at the water rushing past, Cota hoped that Bear would come back.

"Maybe he went to back to the Farm? Maybe he thinks we'll meet in our spot?"

Cota rose to his feet and started to head back to the Farm, but his intuition prevailed.

"Bear will come back. I'm staying here. He knows I can't get across the river."

It rained most of the night. Cota sat upright, beneath the long draping branches of a spruce tree, waiting. His mind said, *run, go find Bear*. His heart said, *stay*. With each passing minute, the waiting grew more and more painful.

By morning, the rain had stopped but overcast skies prevailed.

Cota emerged from beneath the spruce and shook his whole body in a quivering wave, trying to escape both the dampness and his own despair. He walked closer to the edge of the river. Standing on the muddy edge, Cota watched as the river ripped violently past. With all the rain and snow melt, the banks could barely contain the flow.

"No way I'd make it across the river now."

Cota looked up beyond the river, thinking about Bear on the other side. With all the rain, the water continued to rise through the night. The rush of current was so strong he wasn't sure if Bear could even make it back across the raging torrents.

The rumble of brush trampling through the woods startled Cota, and he jumped back, nearly tumbling into the water.

"Bear! I knew you would come back. Thank you! How did you get across the river?"
"I swam," Bear said incredulously. "How do you think?"

Cota looked at Bear, then back at water. The river's fluid swirl was deceiving, but Cota knew, had he tried to swim across, he would be swept downstream with no chance of surviving. Cota looked back at Bear, water still dripping from his thick black coat, and was in awe at the size and strength of an animal that could navigate such a feat.

"I can't believe--"
"Come on, let's go!" Bear interrupted.
"Where?"
"Biggs! I picked up his trail. He came in from the north, and now he's tracking along the river. He's headed for the Farm."
"You came back to get me?" Cota's held tilted sideways as he looked up at Bear with even more amazement, his eyes filled with hope.
"Yes, I knew you would be here. Now come, let's go get

Biggs."

Cota could not believe his ears. Biggs was on his way home, and Bear had found him. Cota smiled as he ran through the woods trailing Bear.

"Where is he?" Cota yelled out, trying to keep up.

Bear didn't answer but kept running. He didn't stop until he got to the point where he had picked up the trail of Biggs's scent.

"He passed through here," said Bear.
"I don't smell it," Cota was confused.
"With all the rain, the scent fades fast. But, I tracked further upstream and when the wind shifted, I caught his scent in the air."

Bear turned, lowered his head and looked Cota in the eyes. "You were right. All this time you knew he was still alive."

Cota did not gloat, or even say a word. He just nodded and said, "let's go get him."

Bear and Cota followed the river upstream. They trekked for miles, and the trail of Biggs was getting stronger. They knew they were getting close, but several times they had to detour away from the river, and the humans that lived nearby. Each time they circled back, they picked up the trail again.

"Biggs is staying true to the river," said Bear. "He knows the way home."
"Yes, but the Farm is on the other side. If he tries to cross the river, he'll drown for sure."
"We need to get to him."

Bear and Cota trailed Biggs's scent up the river all afternoon, worried he might attempt swimming across.

"It will be dark soon," said Cota.
"Look!" Bear stopped abruptly, his long paw raised into the air.

After months and months of searching, Cota's belief that Biggs was alive finally proved true.
"BIGGS!" Cota yelled out to his friend.
But the whoosh of the river drowned out his plea. Biggs was too far away to hear. Both Cota and Bear stood with mouths gaping in disbelief. Looking upstream, they watched as the German shepherd traipsed across the fallen tree that stretched across the river.

"The chain!" Cota said.

The three-feet of wet chain dangled from his collar, swaying with each stride.

Then Bear and Cota watched in horror as the Chain snagged on a broken branch, flipping Biggs into the air. Seconds passed slower than a falling sun as Biggs tumbled awkwardly, clawing desperately at nothing but air. Time vaulted into light speed once Biggs hit the water and the current swept him under, Biggs and the chain disappeared.

Bear and Cota rushed to the edge of the bank. The raging current swept Biggs past them in seconds. Suddenly, he surfaced and Cota caught a glimpse of Biggs's head bobbing and paws churning helplessly.

"BIGGS!" Cota yelled out but to no avail.

Biggs's head bobbed in and out of the water, and the current ripped him past so fast there was nothing either of them could do. Then he was gone.

"The Shallows!" Cota turned and looked at Bear.

Both took off running without another word, knowing their only chance to save Biggs was to get to the Shallows first. The Shallows is long stretch of the river that cuts between open fields on either side. There, the water spreads out across the terrain, weaving through large boulders, before dropping into a series of rapids, leading to the falls. The falls cut through a canyon formed by steep mountain ridges rising on either side.

Bear and Cota both knew the course of the river well, and they knew if they didn't get to the Shallows, Biggs would drown. The Shallows was miles downstream, but the river's course took several long swooping S-turns from where Biggs fell in. The Shallows was just beyond the last turn. If Bear and Cota cut a path straight across, they might make it in time.

But, they would have to scale up and down three big ridges to get there.

Cota was tired and weak, his frail body worn down by age and the grind of surviving the brutal winter. Still, he ran as fast as he could. But Cota could not keep up and soon lost sight of Bear racing up the ridge above him. Cota pressed as hard as he could, but his body was failing him.

Cota knew there was nothing he would be able to do even if he reached the Shallows. The water was too swift. It would be up to Bear to save Biggs. Still, Cota ran with the urgency to help.

As he ran up, then down, then up again, Cota pressed on as fast as his legs would carry him, hoping desperately that Bear would make it to the Shallows in time. Cota's mind raced through all the days and months that he had searched for Biggs. His heart was pounding against the frail walls of his chest, his mind swirling at the brutal twist of fate that brought his friend so close to home, only to be swept away by the torrents.

Cota's mind flashed back to the image of Biggs standing on the fallen tree. Even from a distance, he could tell the German shepherd was worn down, his body beaten by the elements. And the chain. Cota smiled, knowing he was right about Biggs breaking free, and the fact he was still wearing the links of chain. Cota could not wait to hear the stories of Biggs's adventure.

"Bear will save him."

Cota's lungs were about to burst. It had been years since he had run so far in one mad-dash. As he raced down the final ridge, he could see the field leading to the Shallows. Cota had nothing left, but he ran anyway, across the open field and toward the river. With each stride, the raging rapids grew louder, but there was no sign of Bear. Or Biggs.

As Cota neared the river, he should have pulled up and slowed his pace. But he was too excited. The rush of adrenaline that had carried him across the ridges, and to the Shallows could not be contained. Cota dashed over the riverbank and locked his claws into the mud.

The mud, slick as ice, offered no traction. Cota's momentum pushed him down the bank, and into the water. He clawed furiously at the riverbank and cried out for Bear. Bear was upstream, standing atop a bolder, waiting on Biggs. Above the rush of currents, he thought he heard the high-pitched cry of Cota, and turned his head to look, but he could not see the coyote in the water.

Darkness was falling fast, and the mist rising from the river consumed the moment. Seconds passed in rapid-fire. Bear turned back and looked upstream, trying to find Biggs.

The current thrust Cota into a rock and he gripped his claws into a log wedged against the tides. Holding on for life, he could still see the image of Bear, a dark mound silhouette cast against the gray sky, and moving with perfect symmetry. The long black arm swooped into the water, as Bear spun atop the boulder.

The currents swirling around Cota ripped him away from the log and swept him into the whirlpool behind the rock. Cota churned his weary legs with all that he had left, barely keeping his head afloat. With only a hint of light remaining, Cota saw Bear lift Biggs from the raging river and toss him toward the shore. Cota's final vision was the image of Biggs flailing body sailing through the air, and a glistening broken chain swaying like a kite's tail. Cota smiled.

"Biggs you made it home!"

Cota's last words, whisked away by the wind and the thunderous drone of rapids, would never be heard by his friends. His purpose finally found, Cota carried hope and the love of friendship, to the river's end.

ABOUT THE AUTHOR

Joe Cundiff is a writer from southwest Virginia. A love of dogs, and living within the mountains of Appalachia has provided the backdrop and inspiration for this novel. Joe is an avid outdoorsman, hunter, adventurer, and poet. Capturing the essence of all those experiences inspire him to write, and to share the depth of feeling held within each place. This is Joe's first novel.

joecundiff.com